Euge

ne Scribe

A Russian Honeymoon

A Comedy in Three Acts

Euge

`

ne Scribe

A Russian Honeymoon
A Comedy in Three Acts

ISBN/EAN: 9783743324411

Manufactured in Europe, USA, Canada, Australia, Japa

Cover: Foto ©Andreas Hilbeck / pixelio.de

Manufactured and distributed by brebook publishing software
(www.brebook.com)

Euge

ne Scribe

A Russian Honeymoon

A RUSSIAN HONEYMOON

A COMEDY

IN THREE ACTS

ADAPTED BY

MRS. BURTON'HARRISON

From the French of Eugène S

NEW YORK

THE DEWITT PUBLISHING HOUSE

MDCCCXC

SPECIAL NOTICE.

ACTING RIGHTS RESERVED.

———

A RUSSIAN HONEYMOON

SCENE, RUSSIAN POLAND.

TIME 1850.

ACTS FIRST AND SECOND.— A room in the house of Ivan the Shoemaker.

ACT THIRD.— A drawing-room in the Château of the Count Woroffski.

COSTUMES.

ALL RUSSIAN, OF THE TIME OF 1850.

ALEXIS.— Peasant's blouse and trousers trimmed with fur, and at the end of third act full-dress uniform of Russian officer.

POLESKA.— First act, rich traveling dress of velvet and fur; second and third acts, peasant's gala dress.

BARONESS.— First part of third act, rich house-dress; end of act, traveling dress of velvet and fur.

IVAN.— Peasant's blouse, full trousers, high boots.

MICHELINE.— Peasant's dress.

KOULIKOFF.— Blouse and trousers of black velvet edged with fur, fur cap.

OSIP.— Peasant's dress.

CAST OF THE CHARACTERS.

MADISON SQUARE THEATRE,
New York, Monday, April 9, 1883.

ALEXIS PETROVITCH,   -   MR. FREDERIC BRYTON.
A journeyman (afterward Gustave, Count Woroffski).

POLESKA, - - - - - - AGNES BOOTH.
His wife.

BARONESS VLADIMIR,   - - - MISS ADA DYAS.
His sister.

IVAN,   - - - - - MR. W. J. LEMOYNE.
A master shoemaker.

MICHELINE,   - - - MISS ESTELLE CLAYTON.
His daughter.

KOULIKOFF DEMETROVITCH,   MR. MAX FREEMAN.
Intendant of the Château Woroffski.

OSIP,   - - - - - MR. EDWIN ARDEN.
A young peasant.

Guards, Peasants, Ladies, Retainers, etc.

SYNOPSIS.

THE rising curtain discloses the interior of the house of Ivan the Shoemaker. The samovar burns on the table. The lamp burns under the Virgin's picture. A wolf skin is nailed to the wall. High up above the stove, covered with sheepskins, lounges a peasant idly smoking, while others drink around the table, during the hour of recreation. Outside, the snow is falling in thick flakes; inside the log fire is roaring lustily. Wedding bells are chiming; men and maidens clad in gay peasant garments are marching in procession to the church.

Gustave, Count Woroffski, has married Poleska de Fermstein, only to find that early in the honeymoon she develops such traits of temper and pride as will render their married life insupportable, unless he can find some means to subdue her. He accordingly goes before her to an estate, lately become his by inheritance, where he enters the service of a shoemaker, Ivan, under the assumed name of Alexis Petrovitch, and awaits the coming of his wife. Upon her arrival he tells her that he is Alexis, a serf, having married her on a false pretense, and that she, being his wife, is a serf too. He sets her to sew and to spin; he tames her as Petruchio tamed Katharine. She, however, manages to send an appeal to the Count's sister, for protection, and the second act closes with the arrest of Alexis by his own guards. The third act shows a drawing-room in the Château Woroffski, where the Baroness has summoned Poleska to state her wrongs. Poleska obtains from the Baroness an order of separation, and, having obtained it, repents, declares that though her husband is a serf she cannot leave him, finally sees Gustave appear in his true character, and is folded in his arms. Love has conquered pride.

This version of Scribe's pretty comedy was given its first production at the hands of amateurs, and was such an unqualified success that it was soon after staged at the Madison Square Theatre, with an excellent cast, where its popularity was confirmed by large audiences during a very successful run.

The *Critic* in its theatrical notes says: "Of all the pretty plays which have been seen on the boards of the Madison Square Theatre, 'A Russian Honeymoon,' by Mrs. Burton Harrison, is the prettiest."

A RUSSIAN HONEYMOON.

ACT I.

SCENE I.—*(The cottage of Ivan, the shoemaker. Door in flat, C. is open, showing snowy landscape. R. & L. are doors leading to rooms in cottage. Shoemaker's bench and tools, and a half-finished shoe, R. As the curtain rises Ivan, Micheline and journeymen are seen seated at breakfast, L. Alexis seated apart, R.; buried in thought. Country girls come and go C. D., offering Alexis shoes to mend; movement in groups during singing of chorus. Russian stove up L., with peasant lounging on top. At the rising of the curtain a drinking chorus is sung by workmen at table.)*

IVAN *(drinks, sets down glass)*.— Bravo! Bravo! Ah, it does my old heart good. It brings back to me my own youth, when I could sing with the best of you.

(Wedding bells heard in distance.)

MICHELINE *(running to window)*.— Oh, father, see! There go Olga and Michael, on their way to church to be married. Oh! isn't he a beauty!

IVAN.— Fill up, lads, drink to their health. Good luck attend them. *(All laugh and drink. Singing heard outside.)*

MICHELINE.—There, they are coming this way. See! *(Looks out of window and waves her hand.)* Dear little Olga! And to think I'm not even allowed to go to her wedding!

IVAN.— Stop grumbling, girl. These weddings turn all the young heads. Off, lads, to your work!

MICHELINE *(springs upon stool to gaze from window and waves hand)*.— See the fine silver crown Olga's wearing. Yes, father, I'm coming! *(Singing grows louder, bridal procession passes window at back.)* A real gold chain, too. Yes, father, they've gone now. *(Returns from window sighing and busies herself about table.)* I wish it were my wedding day.

(Workmen go off C. D. F. singing.)

IVAN *(going over to Alexis and slapping him on shoulder)*.— Well, my good fellow, are you going to mope there all day, and go hungry?

ALEXIS.— Answer me one question, Master Ivan. Am I paid wages to make merry—or to make shoes?

IVAN.— One doesn't interfere with the other, in my creed. Look at me, for example. Born a serf and a vassal of the Woroffski estate, and consequently a prisoner on this domain, I've managed to build up here in the wilderness a shoe business that, I flatter myself, might hold its own in Warsaw. And my shoes are not made for the country people hereabout, I'll warrant you. They, poor miserable creatures, go barefoot; small encouragement for an artist in my line! But my wares go to Germany, even! Think of it, all Germany demands them; no wonder I work and sing from morning to night. And you'd better believe I've put my hand to more trades than this. Doctoring, hair-dressing, blood-letting—all's one to me. Ah! if you could have seen me pull the miller's tooth yesterday. Ho! ho! ho! roots like radishes! I dragged him out of the chair twice before I got it. Ho! ho! ho! and the rascal wanted to put me off with a fee of ten copecks! So much for the gratitude of human nature. Ho! ho! Why, man, you're as dull as the devil's grandfather!

ALEXIS *(at bench R. coldly).*—Have I not finished the task you set for me this morning?

IVAN *(at C.).*—Certainly. And I haven't a workman in the lot who can beat you. Look at that shoe. *(Takes up Alexis' half-finished work.)* Why, a princess might wear it, let alone a peasant.

ALEXIS *(not looking at Ivan).*—Then, if I have satisfied you, why not let me amuse myself according to my own notions. It is little to ask, I'm sure.

IVAN *(dryly).*—As you like. When the conscience isn't clear, one can't look his neighbor in the face, says the proverb. *(Aside to Micheline.)* He's a perfect bear, that fellow!

MICHELINE *(who has been from time to time striving to attract the attention of Alexis, but without success, at table L., aside to Ivan).*—You are right, father. In the two days since he has been here, nobody has gotten a civil word out of him; or a look either, for that matter. Perhaps the poor man has been unfortunate. Perhaps he isn't satisfied with his pay.

IVAN *(aside, angrily).*—Not satisfied with his pay! Not satisfied with ten copecks a day! Chatter, chatter, when the tongue itches, says the proverb. Why, girl, I pay like a prince, did you but know it. Hold your tongue now, and get about your work. I never knew a matter yet that was improved by a woman's interfering.

> *(Micheline crosses to R. shrugging her shoulders. She manages to drop a bright-colored handkerchief from her neck in passing near Alexis, who, roused from his abstraction, picks it up with great courtesy and restores it, not to its right place, as Micheline stands coquettishly expecting, but to her hand, with a grave bow. Micheline pouts, and goes off discomfited, R. D.)*

IVAN *(who has put on his spectacles to examine Alexis's work, aside).*— He's a workman worth holding to—that's certain. And an employer ought always to be generous, if he finds it to his advantage! *(He again slaps Alexis on shoulder.)* Tell me, my lad, do you belong to this part of the world?

ALEXIS *(coming down R.).*— Yes, Master; I am, like you, a Russian Pole. But I've been knocking about in many countries these five years past.

IVAN.— What for, may I ask?

ALEXIS.— In search of fortune.

IVAN.— Have you found the elusive female?

ALEXIS *(laughing).*— No, in faith. The jade is like all the rest of them. When one sets out in pursuit of her, that's just the time she takes care not to let herself be caught.

IVAN.— The Devil!

ALEXIS.— Not at all! Only a philosopher.

IVAN.— Well, my boy, if you want to stay with me, the affair is in your own hands. You turned up here a couple of days since, and, on the strength of your honest face, I offered you ten copecks a day. But a good workman is like a good shoe, whose value comes out only in the wearing; and the long and short of it is, if you stay I will pay you six copecks additional.

ALEXIS *(cutting leather with knife).*— I have what satisfies me, and that's enough. *(Sighing.)* If I had no worse trouble now——

IVAN *(aside, comically).*— Aha! it's coming. That sigh portends a love scrape. *(Aloud.)* It can't be my daughter Micheline who has been casting sheep's eyes in your direction. That wouldn't suit me at all!

ALEXIS *(going back to bench, smiling).*— Set your mind at rest on that score. I wish with all my heart that I could be in love with your pretty Micheline.

IVAN.— What do you mean by that?

ALEXIS.— I mean that, in my position, Master Ivan, a man, to be reasonable, must love his equal. But then who ever heard of reasonable love?

IVAN.— Marry, come up! Is the fellow mad enough to be sighing for some great lady of the Court?

ALEXIS *(sitting on bench, sadly).*— You have hit the nail on the head now, master. And a lady, who, to my sorrow, is prouder in her own fair self than all the grand-duchesses in Russia.

IVAN *(whistling in derision).*— Whew! In love with a duchess! Perhaps that's what you call reasonable love. I call it madness. Stick to your last, friend Alexis, stick to your last. *(Sound of sleigh-bells at back.)* Look down, not up, if you've got your wits about you. Who comes there? Ah, here's Koulikoff Demetrovitch, the Intendant of my lord's estate.

(*Enter Koulikoff C. D. F. whip in hand, followed by several peasants, who await orders.*)

KOULIKOFF *(cracking his whip and speaking off to followers).*— Hurry up there, louts, and go to their help. Don't stand with your arms crossed staring at me. Shall I go myself. *(Stamping.)* Fifty blows of the knout to the fellow who gets there last. *(Exeunt peasants C. D. F.)* There's no better way of expediting matters than a threat like that, I've found. Ah! good morning, Ivan.

IVAN. — Your servant, Intendant. What's going on without?

KOULIKOFF.— A handsome chariot, four horses, two postillions and one passenger stuck in the mud-hole opposite your door—that's all.

ALEXIS *(starting, aside).*— Poleska! *(Aloud.)* Why couldn't you have said so before, fellow?

(Exit precipitately L. D.)

KOULIKOFF *(strutting about with offended dignity).*— Fellow! fellow! Hum! Pray who is this vagabond you have picked up?

IVAN.— One of my workmen; a rover, returned from the wars. He took the place very recently, but he belongs to the estate; and a treasure I've found in him.

KOULIKOFF *(R.).*— Hum! Can't say much for his manners. Too free, too free, entirely. Don't know his place. What's his name?

IVAN.— Alexis Petrovitch; and a strapping fellow he is, as you see.

KOULIKOFF *(taking snuff, and meditating).*— Petrovitch, Petrovitch. He belongs to us. They are registered in my farm book. He has come back just in time, as I am making up my books. I'll warrant, when my lord the Count comes he'll find affairs in order. During thirty years of faithful service to the estate, I've not sat with folded arms. For one thing, I can't begin to count the knoutings I've administered.

IVAN *(dryly).*— I believe you. *(Aside.)* It is indeed thirty years that we have endured his tyranny. Set the groom on the master's nag and you'll see the dust fly, says the proverb.

KOULIKOFF *(sitting at table)*.— Well, well, that's neither here nor there.   If, in my modest way, I have established a reputation as a disciplinarian, so much the better for me when my lord, the Count, arrives.   Let him come when he will, he shall find the faithful Koulikoff prepared !

IVAN *(aside)*.— He's busy enough ; when he's nothing else to do he scolds the little ones and throws stones at the pigs. *(Aloud.)*   No news in the Commune, Intendant ?

KOULIKOFF.— Times are dull, neighbor.   The usual trifles ; a knouting here and there, to keep my hand in. Olga and Michael married to-day, as you know.   Yesterday, I stood god-father to Marfa's third brace of young ones.   That woman is invaluable to the estate !   To-day I clapped that old hag Fenitcska into prison for setting fire to the cattle shed.   The old fool was trying to drive the fiend out of her cow with a pan of burning charcoal.

IVAN *(aside)*.— Pity somebody couldn't try the same experiment on you, boaster ! *(Aloud.)*   No tidings then of our gracious little father, the Count ?   'Twill be something of a change to the estate, to own a rollicking young soldier for a master, instead of the lamented excellency, his uncle. *(Aside.)*   Good riddance of the old curmudgeon. *(Aloud.)* New blood, new spirit, as the proverb says !

KOULIKOFF.— The estate is in competent hands, my man ; never fear.   Not that I object to the new Count's paying us a visit.   He has never seen the property ; and, at his age, 'tis but natural, and I offer no objections.

IVAN *(curiously)*.— Then we may expect him shortly, Intendant ?   They tell me great doings are going on at the Castle.   The steward ransacking the country side for good things ; and my girl says she'll never in the world have eggs enough for all the housekeeper has ordered.

KOULIKOFF *(with importance)*.— Village babble ! village

babble! One who is in the confidence of the Count must respect himself. I suppose it isn't part of the Intendant's duty to take notice of such idle chatter. Must I tell you all I know, forsooth?

IVAN.— It wouldn't take you long, neighbor.

KOULIKOFF *(confused)*.— Well, well, this much I am at liberty to disclose, friend Ivan *(takes snuff ; Ivan offers to use K's box, but is refused with dignity)*, as you know, the late Count, owing to a quarrel with his brother's family, had never invited any one of them to set foot on the estate. He wouldn't so much as allow the names of his next of kin, Count Gustave and his sister, the Baroness Vladimir, to be mentioned in his presence ; so we have never seen either of them. But for our old master's dying without having left a will, we probably never would. Here, six months after the Count's death, I suddenly receive orders to put the castle in readiness for a visit from the family. For two weeks I have been in hourly expectation of news of their arrival, but not a word has come. Such extravagance! Fresh meat and fowls every day, and cords of the best wood burning to waste in the fireplaces!

IVAN *(horrified)*.— No?

KOULIKOFF.— Yes. It's enough to make the old master come flying back to swear at us!

IVAN *(turning thumb downward)*.— Oh! they've got him safe enough, never fear.   *(Both laugh and chuckle.)*

KOULIKOFF.— Where's your daughter, shoemaker?

IVAN *(rising and putting chair back)*.— Oh! she's at work somewhere. No lazybones when I'm about, Intendant.

KOULIKOFF.— Why don't you marry her off, Ivan? A strapping girl like that might look for the best of husbands. What do you say to me for a son-in-law?

IVAN *(laughing)*.— You, my son-in-law!

KOULIKOFF.— Yes, why not. She's a beauty, that girl.

IVAN.— Excuse me, Intendant, but what a son-in-law you'd make! *(Laughs. Koulikoff is confused.)*

(Enter Micheline running, C. D. F.)

MICHELINE.— Father, dear; such an accident — such a beautiful lady coming in.

(Enter Countess Poleska C. D. F. She is followed by peasants bearing hand-bags, cloaks, etc.; others group at door and window.)

POLESKA *(waving off peasants, also Ivan and Koulikoff who advance, bowing. To peasants)*.— There, that will do. Go back now, and help my servants to regain my possessions. My people have orders to see that you are properly rewarded. Awkward and stupid are no words for it! A splendid road; and the idiots pick out the only mud-hole to upset me in. *(Comes down.)*

MICHELINE *(timidly)*.— Pray, my lady——

POLESKA *(C.)*.— Hold your tongue, girl— And, to crown my misfortunes, the blockheads, in trying to lift my carriage, have broken one of the springs. I am forced to take refuge in this miserable hut. Heaven grant me patience to see the end of it!

MICHELINE *(hesitating)*.— I was only going to say to the lady that it was not entirely the fault of our men. Poor Fedor worked so hard that he has his foot badly crushed for his pains.

POLESKA *(impetuously)*.— Oh, how sorry I am. Poor fellow! Let us hasten to his assistance.

MICHELINE.— Not over these roads, with those fine shoes, my lady.

POLESKA *(rapidly)*.— Yes, you are right. Besides, I could do nothing. What a misfortune! An honest workman, perhaps the father of a family! Let a physician be summoned immediately. Take my purse. Let the man know that I will take care of him. What! does no one stir to obey me?

> *(Micheline carries purse to Ivan; Koulikoff and Ivan exchange looks of astonishment. Ivan goes to C. D. F. and gives orders without; exeunt peasants, C. D. F.)*

KOULIKOFF *(bowing obsequiously and rubbing hands).* —They have this moment gone, my lady. But allow me to say that I should like to know——

POLESKA *(haughtily).*— Pray, who gave you leave to open a conversation with me?

IVAN *(suavely).*— This, my lady, is the Intendant, Koulikoff, and he ought to know——

POLESKA *(with a gesture of impatience).*— He ought to know how to hold his tongue; and you also.

KOULIKOFF *(enraged; aside).*—Was ever heard such insolence?

POLESKA *(to Micheline).*— Tell me, girl, where am I?

IVAN *(approaching, puts Micheline behind him).*—On the estate of the Count Woroffski, my lady, and about a league from his castle.

POLESKA *(starting joyfully).*—On my husband's estate —on my own land!

KOULIKOFF *(cringing).*— What do I hear? Her Excellency then, is the wife of our noble lord Gustave de Woroffski?

IVAN *(takes off apron hurriedly and runs his hands through his hair).*— A Countess in my cottage!

KOULIKOFF *(same air of submission).*—We had been warned, gracious lady, that the Count was about to arrive, but he had not condescended to inform us that his bride would accompany him.

POLESKA *(impatiently)*.— And the Count has not yet come? He was to reach the castle in advance of me, in order to prepare it for my arrival.

(Ivan and Micheline up stage.)

KOULIKOFF.— If the Countess pleases, if such be the case, I have not had the honor of being notified. I am deeply mortified.

(As he speaks, Poleska passes by him and walks to and fro, soliloquizing.)

POLESKA.— My poor Gustave, who would set off before me, to arrange everything to suit my fastidious requirements; I dared not tell him that I had almost as soon forego the state of a reception suited to our rank, as part with him. Soon I shall rejoin him. Oh! What happiness. *(Turns swiftly upon Koulikoff.)* It is all your fault.

KOULIKOFF *(astonished)*.— Mine! Your High Nobility?

POLESKA.— Yes, yours. Are you not the Intendant of this property?

KOULIKOFF *(swelling)*.— For thirty years, Your Excellency, the name of Koulikoff Demetrovitch——

POLESKA *(interrupting)*.— Why in the world, then, don't you keep the road in order? That mud-hole is a disgrace to you. Couldn't you guess that I would be in haste to rejoin my husband? Have you no sense—no judgment? Consider yourself dismissed, upon the spot.

(Turns up stage.)

KOULIKOFF *(with horror)*.— Me! I! Koulikoff Demetrovitch—dismissed!

IVAN *(aside)*.— That woman respects nobody, it is plain. *(Aloud.)* If, until the carriage is repaired, the Countess would honor us by taking some refreshment. Sit down, for good luck, that the chickens and the bees may multiply, says the proverb.

POLESKA *(languidly seating herself at table L.).*—Well, yes, perhaps so. But, to save time, tell them to fetch me only tea and muffins.

ALL.— Tea ! Oh ! yes, my lady, tea !
> *(All rush to table and busy themselves with serving a cup of tea from samovar. Poleska tastes the mixture and refuses it with disgust.)*

POLESKA.— Take this stuff away ! I asked for tea—and muffins.

IVAN *(dismayed).*— Muffins !

POLESKA.— Yes, muffins, toasted and buttered; and a little strawberry jam, perhaps.

IVAN *(in despair).*—Strawberry jam ! I am afraid it will be impossible for us to serve what her Excellency asks for. *(Reflecting.)* There's some prime old cabbage soup, now——

POLESKA *(angrily).*— Impossible ! Nothing is impossible, if I wish it. Let the muffins be brought immediately.

IVAN.— Please your ladyship, we don't exactly know what they are.

MICHELINE *(sorrowfully).*— We have never had any.

POLESKA.— What audacity !

IVAN.— But, my lady——

POLESKA.— He dares object——*(Rises.)* Understand that my word is law ; not even my husband dares oppose me. Heaven made woman to command and man to obey !

MICHELINE *(aside).*— Can this be true ! I wish it were !

POLESKA.— And now, I *will* have muffins.

IVAN *(aside, mimicking Poleska).*— She *will* have muffins.   *(Exit Ivan R. D.)*

KOULIKOFF.— If the Countess will permit herself to take an hour's repose, I fly to my poor dwelling which is near at hand. I shall fetch some tea ; and, at the same time order my kibitka—a little vehicle—which in a short time will enable Madame to rejoin her august bridegroom at the castle.

POLESKA *(joyfully).*— So soon ! With Gustave so soon ! Oh ! you dear, good, nice, kind, comical old thing ; only hurry off, or I shall die of impatience.

KOULIKOFF.— And Madame will deign to give me back my place ?

POLESKA.— That, or some other. I will see what can be done for a reformed Intendant, only fly !

KOULIKOFF.— I go, Madame ; launched like a thunder-bolt at your command. *(Exit Koulikoff C. D. F.)*

POLESKA *(sitting again at table, L.).*— What a piece of work to get what one wants ! And they call Russia a civilized country. Ah ! I am worn out with fatigue, for I have travelled all night.

MICHELINE.— All night, my lady ! you must indeed be tired.

POLESKA.—What would I not have done, to reach him the sooner ? My good, kind husband, who lives but to please me. The three days that I have been away from him seemed an eternity.

MICHELINE *(surprised).*— I thought it was only among poor folks that they marry for love, my lady.

POLESKA.—Love, simpleton ! How should you know the meaning of the word ! Go, girl, and leave me to myself. *(Exit Micheline, courtesying, R. D.)* Yes, three days ! and what have they not taught me. Oh ! Gustave, I shall prove myself worthy of the rank and power you have bestowed on me. Even the peasants, cringing in this miserable hut, show me the homage that awaits me. I, the daughter of a brave officer, whose only dower is her beauty, who from childhood

has dreamed but of shining in the great world. *(Rises.)*
Henceforth I shall reign like a queen. Slaves and vassals
shall bow before me. Equipages, jewels, palaces, are mine
to command. Madame la Comtesse de Woroffski. Ah!
what music to my ears. Ha! who's there? who dares in-
trude on me? *(Enter Ivan R.)*

IVAN.— May it please your ladyship——

POLESKA.— You will best please my ladyship by taking
your ugly face away! Spare me the sight of you! If I am
obliged to remain a while in this hovel, I will try to rest, so
that Gustave may not preceive the marks of fatigue from my
long journey. Let your daughter wait on me. I like the
girl and will take her into my service——

IVAN.— But, Madame——

POLESKA *(stamping her foot).*— Learn once for all, fellow, that I don't know the meaning of a but. If not— *(men-
acing gesture),* you understand?

(She turns imperiously and exit R. D.)

IVAN *(ruefully).*— I understand. *(Sits on bench.)* Ugly
face, forsooth! Ah! yes, I understand that my poor master,
the Count, has got the devil of a temper to deal with! *(Begins
to work.)* Well, here I am, alone like a finger, as the proverb
says, and free to speak my mind. Marry, come up! As
soft as silk, and as fine as a peacock, you'd take her to be—
the vixen! But taste the quality of her temper once! She's
naught but a Baba Yaga.

(Enter Alexis L. D.)

ALEXIS.— Ah! Here you are, Master! And where may
be the lady whose carriage was upset?

IVAN.— The carriage! I'm not so sure but 'twas a mortar
and pestle. That's what our witches ride in, through the air.
(With an anxious look at door R.) The lady! she's in
there. Don't speak so loud, I beg of you. Don't stir her up

again. Oh! If you only met her once, you'd not ask to re-
peat the operation.

ALEXIS *(with a movement toward door R. which he re-
presses).*— I have met her, to my cost! Hark ye, friend Ivan;
do you remember what I told you a while ago about my
hopeless passion? Well, then, I love *her! (He points to
door R.)*

IVAN *(in consternation).*— Man alive, you are mad! You,
a miserable vassal of her lord's estate, dare to cast your eyes
upon his bride! Love her? Love the most wicked, imperi-
ous, haughty creature that ever trod the earth! That is, to
judge from a very brief acquaintance.

ALEXIS *(dryly; putting his hand upon Ivan's shoulder).*
— I have enjoyed a more extensive acquaintance with the
lady. She is my wife! *(Goes up R.)*

IVAN *(looking about for escape, then barricading himself behind table).*— O! Lord! The fellow's raving. I
might have known what it was from the beginning. Oh!

(Alexis retreats to C. D. F. and stands laughing.)

ALEXIS.— Listen to me, Ivan. *(Ivan comes out cau-
tiously L. C.)* Consumed with love for one as high above
me as the moon above the earth, I took the name and rank
of the noble Count de Woroffski, who was expected to visit
Buda, where she lived. A small inheritance recently coming to me, together with the savings of six years past, suf-
ficed to sustain my assumed position. I married her—I can
say no more. *(He turns his head away.)*

IVAN.— Matrimony is sure to bring down a fellow's spirit,
sooner or later. But how in the mischief came you to journey hither on your honeymoon?

ALEXIS.— The newspapers announced that the Count de
Woroffski had recently inherited a principality on the bor-
ders of Russia and Poland. My wife urged me to visit this

spot by way of a wedding journey; and I, remembering the home of my humble ancestors, was glad of an excuse to leave Buda and the embarrassments of my false position there.   An explanation with her I had deceived could not be much longer deferred; and it were better three hundred leagues away from her home and family.   Thus a strange chance has led me back among my own people.   I, who am but a poor devil of a workman, a slave, as you say, bring with me a bride by birth and education far above me.   From this point, Ivan, there is no drawing back.   Poleska must know all, and that without delay.   I have faced fire, in my day, as bravely as another, I suppose; but, at this crisis, Master Ivan, I'm afraid!

IVAN *(shrugging).*— Small blame to you, comrade. She'll inform upon you before the Count, no doubt; and you'll be hung in quick order.   Just as little ceremony as she used in dismissing our worthy Koulikoff.   Ah! she's a rare one. *(Grimace toward door R.)* I'd like to wager that she'll bestow on you a larger piece of her mind, in one half hour, than my dear departed managed to give me, during fifteen years of matrimony—and mine was never backward, heaven rest her soul!

ALEXIS *(impatiently).*— Enough, enough, Ivan.   What I dread most, I will own, is——

IVAN *(interrupts).*— The explosion!   I believe you, my boy.   Make peace with heaven when the petard is launched, says the proverb.

ALEXIS.— Ivan, you are a father, you have a feeling heart; I've an act of friendship to impose on you.   If you could only—very delicately—very adroitly—and without giving her too much pain—prepare the way for me——

IVAN *(promptly).*— With the greatest of pleasure in the world, my dear fellow; believe me, the greatest pleasure.

(Aside.) I mustn't show my feelings too plainly—but oh! what an opportunity for getting even with the little spitfire. *(Grimaces toward door R. Aloud.)* As you say, the awl cannot be hidden in the sack much longer, and murder will out.

ALEXIS *(who has been drawing near to and withdrawing from door R.).*— How dare I risk it? See here, Ivan, old fellow; but a moment since, I had my proud falcon tamed, hooded, and resting on my wrist. If I but draw the bandage from her eyes—with the speed of light she will be off.

IVAN *(puzzled).*— She is a high-flyer and no mistake. *(Aside.)* He can't be changing his mind about it. *(Aloud.)* Leave it to me, friend Alexis. Leave it to me. I know womankind, and the way to deal with them. I have a feeling heart——

ALEXIS *(with emotion).*— Be gentle with her, Ivan! Remember her youth, her solitude—her isolation! Treat her as though it were your own child who had come to you in sorrow.

IVAN.— Trust me to forget nothing, my gallant bridegroom. Now, I must be off. I've a little business to attend to, before I inform my lady the Countess of her changed position. *(Movement of Alexis to interrupt.)* Oh! if it's to say you don't want to trouble me, Alexis, don't mention it. I don't mind trouble. I like trouble, when it's for a friend. Better get to work again, my boy; you'll need all you can make to keep your wife in silks and fineries. Ho, ho, ho; The Countess! What a joke! And Koulikoff, ho! ho! ho! Wait till you see his face! Koulikoff! That's the best of all! *(Going off.)* I wouldn't give up this little commission for fifty copecks; shoot me, if I would! *(Exit C. D. F.)*

ALEXIS *(at door R.).*— At last alone ! Oh ! how hard it is to sustain this borrowed character. The deceit is abhorrent to me. Better in truth to be an humble shoemaker than a nobleman who to his wealth and rank alone owes the affection of his wife. Now I am resolved—I will be firm. Rude though the test may be, Poleska shall confront it. Heaven send that her proud spirit may bend now, or the life that is in store for us will be one enduring misery. *(Chorus heard without, Alexis looks C. D. F.)* There is the music of the wedding festival! Yonder goes the bride, hanging upon her husband's arm! He, honest fellow, knows nothing of the pangs that rack my jealous breast. I, the bridegroom of a week, Gustave de Woroffski, lord of these village folk, owner of this vast estate—and husband of a wife I dare not trust.

> *(The bridal procession passes. Chorus and wedding chimes. Alexis stands at window, moodily watching the passers-by.)*

Curtain.

ACT II.

(The cottage as before, table cleared. Micheline comes in on tip-toe R. D.)

MICHELINE.— Oh! dear, one ought to have five pairs of hands and as many feet, to do my lady's bidding. Lucky that she's all tired out with her travelling, and has gone to sleep—as peaceful as the wax baby in the Christmas manger. Heigh ho! It's only a princess born that can take time to sleep at noonday!

(She puts wood in stove L. Enter Osip C. D. F.)

MICHELINE.— Oh! it's you, is it?

OSIP.— How now, my damsel fair, always busy? Come, let's be friends again. Say but the word, and I'll kiss you as soon as wax my thread.

MICHELINE *(laying fresh cloth on table L.)*.—Indeed, you'll do nothing of the kind, Master Osip. Who wants to kiss a cross face like yours? Why, it's as long as our donkey's, and about as cheerful.

OSIP.— Pretty talk from a man's promised wife, isn't it. It's a shame, I tell you. Your head's just turned by these strangers coming here, and my lady taking notice of you. And ever since that fellow Alexis crossed the door-sill, you've treated me like the dirt under your feet.

MICHELINE.— Now, never mind Alexis, there's a good

fellow. You're in such a temper. Maybe you were bitten by a mad dog on the way!

OSIP.— And then, after joking and flirting with every new-comer, you expect me to dance like a puppet when you pull the string.

MICHELINE.— When *you* dance, it will be more like a bear than a puppet! Go on!

OSIP.— Oh! I could go on for a week if——

MICHELINE *(laughing)*.—Don't do that, please. Find something new to say.

OSIP *(angrily)*.—I'll find something new to say when you give me something new to talk about—so, there!

MICHELINE.— Come, Osip, dear, quiet down a bit, and I'll try to mend my ways; what is it you want of me, any-way?

OSIP.— I want you to say you love me.

MICHELINE *(coquettishly)*.— And haven't I said so once, you greedy fellow.

> *(He extends his arms; she appears to lean toward him, then glides under his arm, and crosses stage laughing.)*

OSIP.— There! that's always the way! I, that buy you ribbons from every fair, and gewgaws from every peddler! Haven't I almost broken my neck a-climbing in the tree-tops to fetch you birds' eggs? Do I ever look at the miller's Olga, for all she makes up to me on Sundays; and she called the beauty of the village!

MICHELINE.— The miller's Olga is a horrid, forward thing!

OSIP.— Well, she's pleasanter than some I could name. I might as well butt my head against a wall, as follow you; you're as cold as any frog.

MICHELINE.— If I was made a frog, I can't unmake myself ; and you're very rude to call me names. *(Weeps.)* I shouldn't think you'd want to be married to a fr-fr-fr-og !

OSIP *(consoling her).*— Oh ! Yes I do. Don't cry now, and when the peddler comes again, see what I'll get for you.

MICHELINE *(still sobbing).*— Is it a pair of silk stockings like my lady's, Osip ?

OSIP.— Whatever you say, my girl, if you're only kind to me, the way you used to be.

MICHELINE.— Yes, before we loved each other, Osip ! It was a great deal nicer then ! Well, well, you silly fellow, I'll try, very hard, and perhaps love will come,—the way one falls asleep, without knowing how ! Only, do stop being so jealous. Is it my fault the men run after me ? Would you have me take a stick to my admirers ?

    (Ivan enters C. D. F., during this speech, and stands behind the lovers, his stick raised.)

OSIP.— There's more than one of those fellows that would be the better for a beating. There's Koulikoff Demetrovitch, forever eyeing you on the sly, the ugly old tyrant. And Alexis—I'll spoil his pretty face for him, the coxcomb ! And Peter—and Marko—and Nicholas-of-the-herd, and——

IVAN *(bringing down stick upon Osip's back).*— And Osip ! And Osip ! And Osip ! What, what, is this the way you idlers waste my time ? Your turn next, my lass.

MICHELINE *(shrinking).*— Oh ! father, pray don't. Here comes Koulikoff Demetrovitch, and my lady will be stirring.

    (Osip runs out C. D. F., and, in view of audience, runs into Koulikoff, who is seen through window, carrying a covered tray. Exit Micheline R. D.)

IVAN *(gesticulating towards Poleska's door R.).*— My lady ! My lady ! If she'd take my advice, the Countess would be in no haste to leave her room ! *(Sits at bench.)*

KOULIKOFF *(entering with tray C. D. F.).*— Here I am, fairly dripping. *(Wipes his face.)* By the greatest good luck I found, at home, some tea that I bought of the last caravan ; and here are my prettiest cups.

(He lays table with knife, fork, plates, tea things, etc. Ivan seats himself negligently at table.)

IVAN.— Come, come, Intendant, if you had only known what I know, you might have spared your wind and your pains.

(Noise in room R. Enter Micheline hastily R. D.)

MICHELINE.— Oh, dear father, if you would only hurry with the breakfast. The Countess is awake and is calling for her servants. She says we shall all be knouted because there is no bell in her room.

IVAN *(crossing to table L. ; contemptuously).*— There's the big bell that calls our workmen up, let her try that.

KOULIKOFF *(walking R. hurriedly).*— Pray, my good girl, say from me to the Countess that I have done my best. The tea is served and the little sleigh I promised her is even now at the door.

(He looks up to find that Ivan has helped himself to a cup of tea and is drinking it and smacking his lips.)

KOULIKOFF *(angrily).*— Hollo there ! What in the devil are you about ?

IVAN.— Tasting her tea, as you may see. You're right ; it's capital stuff, and I drink to her health.

MICHELINE *(alarmed).*— Tasting my lady's breakfast ! Oh, father, what will become of us ?

KOULIKOFF *(infuriated).*— What profanation ! Fellow, do you know with how many blows of the knout you'll pay for this joke ?

(Poleska's voice from room R.). — Micheline, Micheline.

MICHELINE *(wringing her hands).*— Oh, father, do get up! If she should come out now and see you! Yes, my lady, coming. *(Exit Micheline R. D.)*

IVAN *(doggedly).*— And pray why should I get up in the presence of a workman's wife, my workman's wife?

KOULIKOFF *(lifting hands).*— His brain is turned by so much honor to his house!

IVAN.— Not at all. You were never more mistaken. It is *she (points with thumb over shoulder to R. D.),* who owes *me* respect. This would-be sovereign is no more the wife of our Count than my daughter is.

KOULIKOFF.— Is this true? Not a Countess! *(Running to door C. D. F.)* Hollo there, Michel, you may drive my sleigh back to the stable.

IVAN.—She's nothing but the wife of Alexis Petrovitch, my journeyman, and a serf on the Woroffski estate.

KOULIKOFF *(piously).*— The Lord forgive her for a lying jade. But how can one be sure of anything?

IVAN.— I have it from Alexis himself.

KOULIKOFF.— The wife of a serf? And she takes the liberty of being hungry and thirsty! Bah! I'm hungry and thirsty. You're hungry and thirsty. Permit me, friend Ivan.

> *(He sits at table and pours out tea ; they simultaneously attack the food. Loud discordant bell rings off R.)*

IVAN *(tranquilly, with mouth full).*— That's the alarm bell for her breakfast. Let her ring!

> *(Door R. opens. Enter Poleska like a whirlwind, followed by Micheline. Both men keep their seats, laughing insolently.)*

POLESKA.— Was ever such impertinence? To keep *me* waiting like this. I who never wait. I who have not yet breakfasted.

KOULIKOFF *(over his shoulder; taking a bite).*— That's exactly my case. Ho! ho!

POLESKA *(trembling with rage).*— What do I see ? To your feet, barbarians, and remember where you are.

IVAN.— Take it easy, good wife, take it easy. Less strife, long life, says the proverb. Always keep your temper—always—especially while fasting. Ho! ho! ho!

MICHELINE.— Great heavens ! My lady, my father is surely mad. *(Aside.)* He will never be allowed to live after this.

POLESKA.— I will give them a lesson in respect.

> *(She passes swiftly between the men, twitches the napkin on which the breakfast is laid, and drags it away. Everything crashes to the ground.)*

KOULIKOFF *(dancing with angry excitement).*— My best Nankin cups. Oh! my beautiful dishes ! Her husband shall pay for this.

POLESKA.— I will pay you on the spot. *(She boxes his ears.)* In one hour both of you shall be hanged.

KOULIKOFF *(rubbing his cheek).*— Ah ! ha ! Madame, you shall sing a different song when the Count hears of your assault upon his honored Intendant ; you shall see, then, how in this part of the world we punish a disobedient and rebellious vassal.

POLESKA *(scornfully).*— A vassal !

KOULIKOFF.— Yes, a vassal. For that's what you are, in spite of your grand ways. You're no more of a Countess than I am—and *(to audience)* I look like a Countess, don't I ?

MICHELINE.— What can this mean ?

IVAN *(triumphantly).*— It means, my girl, that this young woman is not married to our Count de Woroffski, but to Alexis Petrovitch, his serf and my journeyman ; a gallant young fellow, and too good for her, according to my way of thinking. (*Poleska makes a movement of horror, and stands gazing at him with dilated eyes.*) He married her in Buda the other day, under false pretenses to be sure ; but I think any eye witness would allow he has got his punishment already. If you don't believe me, here he comes. Koulikoff, Micheline, let us leave the happy couple to themselves. I've no fancy for remaining on the battle field, when shot and shell are flying about my ears.

(*Exeunt Ivan and Koulikoff R. D. bowing with mock solemnity ; Micheline going last, looking back with sympathy ; Ivan drags her angrily away.*)

POLESKA (*at table L.*).— Oh ! my husband, why are you not here to protect your wife against the insolence of these barbarians ; against dangers which I do not understand ?

(*Enter Alexis C. D. F. He comes slowly up behind her.*)

ALEXIS.— Poleska !

POLESKA (*hearing his voice, turns with delight, offering to throw herself in his arms*).— Oh ! Gustave !

(*He makes no movement in return, but stands with folded arms before her.*)

POLESKA (*perceiving his peasant's dress, utters a cry and staggers*).— Gustave ! It is true then ! Great Heavens ! And I live !

(*Alexis starts forward as if to take her in his arms, but restrains himself and stands with bent head as before.*)

(*Poleska catches at chair behind her and faces him, one hand holding her heart, her breath coming rapidly.*)

ALEXIS.— Yes, Poleska, it is true. You see before you a man whose love for you conquered his reason. Too poor and lowly to dream of winning you in my own estate, I was madly tempted to borrow from another the semblance of those advantages that might make me, in your sight, your peer. Now that you know my crime, judge me ; not as Gustave, your lordly lover—but as Alexis, your guilty husband, who adores you, yet dares not take your hand.

POLESKA *(wildly)*.— Oh ! No, never, never ! Leave me, sir. You—a peasant—a serf—a vile impostor ! Oh, my father ; could you but know the degradation of your child ! What punishment could be found that would equal such a crime ?

ALEXIS.— In your country, death ! Knowing that, as I did, confess that I loved you to risk it ? For be he lord or peasant, the man who risks his life to gain the object of his devotion proves that his love is real.

POLESKA.— Love ! The love of a serf ! What love could give you the right to ally yourself to one of us ?

ALEXIS.— You are the child of an officer who, without birth or fortune, has attained his present rank by bravery and personal merits alone. I, too, have served as he did—a Polish soldier fighting under the banner of France ! If at the close of the campaign I resumed my former means of gaining a livelihood, why should I blush for it ? The money I had laid up was sufficient for my wants, till, in an evil hour, I met you. That day I knew that I was poor ! Why had I not treasures, palaces, equipages, jewels to lay at your feet ? The Count de Woroffski would have shared with you his fortune—more he could not do. I gave you my all. For you I have sacrificed everything, my future—my life, perhaps. In return, punish me if you will, pardon me if you can,—but, pity me, Poleska.

POLESKA *(after a minute of silence, without looking at him)*.— Go !

ALEXIS *(beseechingly)*.— Poleska !

POLESKA.— Call me no more by name. I owe allegiance to the noble Count de Woroffski. None to the slave, Alexis.

ALEXIS *(in a changed tone)*.— One moment, Madame ; in marrying me then, you thought only of my wealth and titles?

POLESKA.— You are free to suppose so.

ALEXIS.— I appeal to your heart. Try to remember how many times you said that none of these mere externals could add to or take from your tender wifely love. "Gustave" you murmured to me—"if fate had placed you in the lowest rank, my heart would have owned you only."

POLESKA *(catching her breath)*.— That—that was said to one I still could respect.

ALEXIS *(proudly)*.— Enough ! Love can bear all but scorn. And now, since it is the moment for revelation, let me say to you, Madame, that, in whatever condition of life you might be placed, a nature like yours would make the misery of your husband.

POLESKA *(throwing back her head)*.— Mine !

ALEXIS.— Yes, yours. Until now, I have schooled myself to bear with your scornful pride ; but, after all, I am your husband ; and I assert my authority.

POLESKA *(indignantly)*.— You have no authority. The marriage is not valid.

ALEXIS *(slowly and decisively)*.— Our marriage holds. The contract which you cared not to examine, bears the simple name of Alexis Petrovitch—soldier and shoemaker—and you, like your husband, are a slave of the Count de Woroffski.

POLESKA *(fiercely)*.— It is false ! I am free ! I obey nobody.

ALEXIS.— Excepting me, your lord and master. Until now I have entreated. Now I command—

(Enter Ivan and Micheline C. D. F. and come down softly.)

POLESKA *(satirically)*.— What you command, sir, is absolutely without importance in my eyes.

ALEXIS *(continuing as if she had not spoken)*.— and you will obey.

POLESKA *(folding her arms disdainfully)*.— That, we shall see.

IVAN *(interrupting)*.— Hollo there ! A row in the household already ?

ALEXIS.— Not at all, master. My wife is submitting with the best grace in the world.

IVAN *(raising hands and eyes)*.— Then a miracle has been worked, that is all !

ALEXIS *(sarcastically)*.— Yes, a miracle. And now, good master, instead of one servant you will have two. My wife will help Micheline at her housework.

POLESKA.— Housework !

ALEXIS *(coldly to Poleska)*.— And you will ask Micheline to kindly lend you some clothes more suitable to your changed fortunes. Micheline, my good girl, I am sure you will oblige my wife.

POLESKA *(scornfully)*.— Your wife !

MICHELINE *(timidly)*.— My Sunday best is at your service, my lady ; and Nika says the blue bodice is quite lovely.

POLESKA *(crossing R.)*.—Poleska de Fermstein stoop to wear a peasant's garb ? Really, sir, your insults are accumulating.

(Ivan attempting to pat her on the shoulder, is fiercely repulsed by Poleska ; Alexis makes a

threatening movement toward Ivan, unseen by Poleska, who drops exhausted upon bench R. covering her eyes with her hands).

IVAN.— Ta! Ta! Ta! good wife. Is that the way for a bride to talk in her honeymoon? I see you are not acquainted with our honest Muscovite fashion of settling such connubial difficulties. It's an old saying, friend Alexis, that a dog, a wife, and a walnut tree, the more you beat them the better they'll be. Allow me to recommend it. The method is rarely know to fail among us. Ah! if you had only seen my dear departed. She knew how to take a husband's chastisement, good soul.

MICHELINE *(kneeling at Poleska's side).*— Yes, and 'twas said the last one made an end of her.

POLESKA *(bursting into tears).*— Oh! what savages are these among whom I have fallen!

(Micheline comforts her.)

ALEXIS *(to Ivan angrily).*— Hold your tongue, master; you go too fast. Come, come, wife, you must obey more promptly. Go at once with Micheline into your chamber.

POLESKA *(rising confronts him).*— I will not go.

ALEXIS.— You will go.

POLESKA *(faltering a little).*— I—I will not.

ALEXIS *(imperatively and with a threatening gesture).* —You shall go at once—or——

POLESKA *(impetuously).*— Yes, I go; but of my own free will, remember. I go, to avoid insult from one I despise. Could I ever again be glad, it would be to free myself from your detestable presence.

(Exit R. D. followed by Micheline.)

IVAN *(aside, rubbing his hands gleefully).*— It's her turn, now, the little spitfire! *(Aloud.)* I congratulate you, my boy. Well done, for a beginning!

ALEXIS *(up C.).*— Yes, it is well done, considering that I have the chill of death in my heart. Never mind, having begun, I'll go on.

IVAN.— That's the spirit. A little perseverance, and all will go well.

(Noise as of furniture upset heard off R.)

ALEXIS.— Don't mind it. It is only my wife at her toilet.

IVAN *(with a shrug).*— Lively times, aren't they? As I was going to say, your only danger lies in the chance of her family taking up cudgels in her behalf.

ALEXIS.— It was for that reason that I brought her here, safely beyond the reach of their vengeance. And now, since I am resolved to settle in these parts, what do you say to selling me this cottage, with the furniture and tools, as it stands?

IVAN *(up C.).*— Willingly, my boy. You are a capital workman, and a worthy fellow. You'll find the cottage comfortable; and, after all, there's no reason why you should not enjoy life here, when you've got your wife in harness. The things are not new, but they are serviceable. Look at that stove. There you can lie and smoke your pipe in peace, while she sweeps, chops the fire wood, hoes the barley patch, rubs the horse down, or performs various other little duties of the kind.

ALEXIS *(laughing).*— That's a fair division of labor now, isn't it?

IVAN.— Oh! We Muscovites know how to make women pay for the salt in their porridge. These benches are heirlooms. They belonged to my father's great grandfather. This table was bought brand new at the Bazaar—fifteen years ago. Then there's the old red cow, she that was sprinkled with holy water by the priest, last St. George's

Day; you might call her lean, but it's in the breed. Let me see—I'll throw in the cow and the good-will of the shop, for—I always like to be generous—suppose we were to fix the price at a thousand roubles, hey?

ALEXIS.— That's generous, certainly—to yourself.

IVAN.— Bah! That's no price at all for one who has been a wealthy nobleman.

ALEXIS *(with an air of severity).*— But for a poor workman, Master Ivan?

IVAN *(at R. eyeing him curiously).*— It appears to me he hasn't parted with everything belonging to his former estate. A hint is as good as a thump, says the proverb.

ALEXIS *(resuming his air of good fellowship).*— Agreed, Master; a thousand roubles be it. I have sent our carriage, the lady's maid and lackeys who accompanied my wife upon her journey, back to Wilna. From the sale of my equipage I will pay the money you demand.

IVAN.— Agreed. And may God give you health and the rank of General, friend Alexis.

(More noise heard off R. Micheline runs in R. D. which is slammed after her with violence.)

MICHELINE.— Oh, what a time. You will never in the world be able to manage her, Alexis. All the chairs and tables knocked over, two new pitchers broken, our beautiful plaster cast of the Kremlin smashed. And I telling her, all the while, how angry father will be.

IVAN.— Angry. And what is it you know, boaster, except to go to merry-makings and set traps for a husband. I am never angry. Besides I have just concluded the sale of all those things to Alexis Petrovitch, here.

ALEXIS *(laughing).*— You can afford to be philosophical, Master.

MICHELINE.— And when I gave her my beautiful Sunday

clothes that Nika made—they are perfectly new, and fitted her as if they had been made for her—she dashed them on the floor, and trod on them. Sooner than work, she said, she'd starve herself, and then she would at least have the pleasure of getting you hanged.

IVAN.— The malice of a wife.

MICHELINE.— Then she saw two of our workmen talking under her window; she uttered a cry of joy, pushed me to the door, slammed it in my face, and then——

IVAN.— She'll never submit, not she.

ALEXIS.— I fear not—see, the door is opening—here she is. Leave us!

IVAN *(going)*.— Come along, Micheline. You'd better try the good old Muscovite custom, Alexis. Beat your furs on feast days and your wife on all days, says the proverb.

> *(He makes the motion of beating. Alexis frowns and pushes him from the room. Exeunt Micheline and Ivan L. D. Enter Poleska R. D. dressed as a Russian peasant.)*

POLESKA *(speaking off R.)*.— Quick! Quick, and you shall have ten roubles for your pains. Die! Ah, no. It were sweeter far to live and be avenged.

> *(Crossing Alexis without looking at him.)*

ALEXIS *(at R. surveying her with admiration)*.— I am enchanted by your submission. Really, you gain by it more than you dream of. The costume suits you to perfection.

POLESKA *(at L. over her shoulder)*.— Indeed.

ALEXIS.— May I ask with whom you were conversing just now?

POLESKA *(over her shoulder)*.— Certainly. A young peasant I had summoned beneath my window to do an errand for me.

ALEXIS *(courteously).*— And the errand?

POLESKA *(meaningly).*— You shall know, in time.

ALEXIS.— I am satisfied to wait. And now, my dear, the day is passing by ; you have assumed your peasant garb, suppose we set to work.

POLESKA.— I work? I stoop to work?

ALEXIS *(gently).*— No one stoops to honest labor. I may as well tell you that I have just bought this little property from Ivan. We are at home, you see. A tiny place, but weather-tight ; we will pass many a cosy winter's evening here. Suppose you begin by putting things to rights, my dear. A peasant's wife must learn to know the use of this, for instance. *(He holds out to her a broom from R.)*

POLESKA *(with an outburst).*— No, I refuse ! I—

> *(Alexis again offers her the broom, with a bow, as in the minuet de la cour ; Poleska looks at him with scorn, then snatches the broom from his hand, and falls to sweeping angrily. She lifts the shoes disdainfully, and ends by throwing them wildly in every direction, some grazing Alexis, till he takes refuge on the stove, laughing.)*

ALEXIS *(aside).*— What a pretty, trim figure, and how the rich blood mantles her cheek at the unwonted exercise ! *(Aloud as Poleska sinks exhausted on chair L.)* Well done, well done, my dear ; and now, as a peasant's wife is never idle, here is another task awaiting you.

> *(He goes back and lifts a spinning wheel from its corner. Poleska repulses him scornfully. Alexis makes a gesture enjoining obedience. She restrains herself with extreme effort.)*

POLESKA *(aside).*— Revenge is close at hand. Ah, why can I not be satisfied to bide my time. *(Aloud, while Alexis is placing the spinning wheel in front of her.)* It is impossible for me to refuse anything so courteously requested.

ALEXIS *(going back to shoe-bench and resuming work, with an air of satisfaction).*— This is as it should be.

> *(He begins the verse of a merry song, Poleska irritated by his cheerful air, works by fits and starts, tangles her thread, finally rises, takes out the distaff, tears off the flax and throws it at his feet. Alexis rises, taking a fresh distaff with flax nicely arranged from the corner, goes toward Poleska, sets wheel in order, and laying his hand on her shoulder, gently compels her to resume her seat.)*

ALEXIS *(smiling).*— Try again, won't you? The second time is more likely to be a success.

POLESKA *(resigning herself).*— You are really too obliging. So much courtesy and high bred grace are hardly to be looked for in a serf.

> *(Alexis bows, returns to bench, and resumes his song. Poleska spins rapidly, then furiously fast. Very soft music here, and off and on till the end of Act III.)*

ALEXIS *(dropping his work and watching her).*— Take care, pray, you will wound your hand. That pretty hand belongs to me, remember. It is my chief treasure, and I guard it with my life.

> *(Makes a movement toward her.)*

POLESKA *(drawing back nervously).*— You forget yourself, sir.

ALEXIS *(smiling and resuming bench).*— No, I do not, Madame. *(Sadly.)* Yes, it is mine, struggle as you may, Poleska. Do you know that while sitting here watching you, I am foolish enough to think that even in this poor, sordid place we may be happy if you will it so. It is our own, this humble home, and here the distractions of the great world can never come to us. In that world, a wealthy nobleman belongs to his duties, to the public—his wife to society—to her pleasures. They have hardly time to love each other, as we may, Poleska. *(He gradually draws nearer to her. Poleska sits, with drooping head and hands crossed in her lap.)* Think of it only, dearest, as I do. Look through my eyes into the future, and see yourself, exiled from the Court, to be sure, but enshrined in a loving heart forever. I will work for you, I will spare you all pain, I will worship you, loving as man never loved before——

> *(String music, tremolo, during this scene. He kneels beside her and puts his arms around her. Poleska starts violently, upsetting wheel. She springs from her chair and motions him away.)*

POLESKA *(agitated).*— Go, go, I cannot bear it. *(With her former cold manner.)* Go back to your work.

> *(A noise outside. Enter Ivan and Micheline running C. D. L. Workmen, peasants, etc., follow.)*

IVAN.— Bad luck, bad luck, Alexis. Let us fly at once. The guards already surround the house. This way, by Madame's chamber window. You and I are to be made prisoners, perhaps hung, to satisfy that little spitfire wife of yours. Oh, Alexis Petrovitch, this never would have happened, had you begun in time to practice Muscovite customs.

MICHELINE *(darting back from R. D. where she has gone to look for a way of escape).*— Too late! Too late. The way is cut off. Oh, Alexis! Oh, my poor, old father!

ALEXIS *(at R. C. calmly).*— This is your work, Poleska.

POLESKA *(standing L. her head thrown back triumph-antly).*— This is my work, Alexis Petrovitch.

(Enter Koulikoff, with guards C. D. F.)

KOULIKOFF.— I'm very sorry, gentlemen, but my orders from the Castle are imperative, and admit of no delay.

IVAN *(crouching on bench, Micheline at his side; rue-fully).*— And what will they do with me, neighbor Kouli-koff?

KOULIKOFF *(at R. C. shrugging his shoulders).*— Hang-ing is suggested; but knouting may be accepted in its stead. *(Ivan winces.)*

ALEXIS *(at L. C.).*— At least, Intendant, you will explain the nature of the charge? What is our offense?

KOULIKOFF *(shrugs shoulders again).*— Offense? Oh, that's neither here nor there, when I have orders from the Castle. Say abduction, say conspiracy, say illegal detention of this female here. Who knows. Not Koulikoff. For thirty years it has been my habit to apply punishment to the serfs whenever the least opportunity offered. Let no man cross the path of Koulikoff when in pursuit of duty. Guards!

(Guards make forward movement.)

ALEXIS *(waves guards back).*— One moment, my good men—*(Draws near Poleska L.)* You have avowed this to be your act, Poleska. Then, be the consequences what they may, I submit. But a moment since, I was fond enough—fool enough—to dream that your heart felt a thrill answering to mine. How bitterly I deceived myself. At that very time you were counting the moments to elapse be-fore I should be torn from your side forever. Farewell! Think sometimes, not alone of the shame and ignominy of the lot to which you have condemned me *(he draws nearer).* but of my changeless love.

POLESKA.— Go! *(She waves him away. Alexis goes.*

then returns with impetuous movement ; guards crossing bayonets to bar his way.)

ALEXIS.—Poleska ?

(Poleska draws herself up to her full height, and points to the door. Guards close around Alexis and lead him away. Tableau. Curtain. As curtain rises on recall, stage is cleared of peasants, soldiers, etc. Alexis seen without in custody of guards. Poleska makes movement toward him with outstretched arms C. Tableau.)

Guard.

Alexis.

Guard.

Micheline, Koulikoff.   *Poleska.*

Ivan.

Curtain.

ACT III.

(A drawing-room in the Château Woroffski, richly furnished, with furs, etc. Doors R. L. and C. in flat, sofa R., arm chairs, writing table, etc. Koulikoff is discovered arranging the furniture.)

KOULIKOFF.— At last everything is ready. Ouf! Since her arrival here, that little Baroness has kept me on the trot. What with her maids, and her lackeys, her pages and her pug dogs, her travelling cat and her travelling doctor, I've got my hands full! Orders and counter-orders, till my brain is fairly buzzing! And the work I've had to get our people in training. All hurrying and scurrying, hither and thither, everybody asking at once what he is to do. I've cut it short by ordering every man Jack of them to keep in the place I've given him, and not to stir from it if he don't want a taste of the lash. Trust Koulikoff to keep the idle vagabonds in order. *(Enter Micheline L. D.).*

MICHELINE *(pleadingly)*.— God be with you, neighbor. I've been looking for you everywhere to ask if you won't help us a bit in our trouble. I know we can depend on you to say a good word for my father to the Baroness.

KOULIKOFF *(aside)*.— She's changed her note, the pretty

pigeon. *(Aloud.)* Young woman! On one thing you may rely. If anybody can succeed in influencing the Baroness, in your behalf and that of your unfortunate father, you have done well to apply to Koulikoff Demetrovitch.

MICHELINE *(joyfully).*— Oh! how lucky that we have a friend in you. How good you are, Intendant.

KOULIKOFF.— So it is said! so it is said! but perhaps they flatter me.

MICHELINE.— Only get my poor old father set at liberty, and I'll be grateful to you forever.

KOULIKOFF *(aside).*— Now's my chance. *(Aloud.)* Do you know, Micheline, for a long time past I've been wanting to ask a favor of you?

MICHELINE.— Of me?

KOULIKOFF *(drawing near to Micheline who retires).* — Yes, of you, pretty one. Don't be afraid, it's only your advice.

MICHELINE *(with importance).*— Oh, my advice! Dear heart, you're welcome to *that.*

KOULIKOFF *(both at R. H.).*— Yes; give your whole mind to the subject, if you please. Fix your close attention on what I am about to say. *(Micheline nods assent.)* In the first place, in giving me an answer, you must promise not to flatter me, but to speak your mind quite frankly. *(Micheline nods again.)* In these days a good wife is not so easy to find, eh, Micheline? *(Micheline nods, but draws away from him.)* *(Drawing nearer.)* One of the kind that are up early at the wheel, that dust and sweep till the house is like a honey-comb. A tidy girl who runs about singing at her work; eh, Micheline? *(Micheline draws away, Koulikoff following her.)* They say it is harder still to find a good husband; a hale, hearty man, not young enough to be a fool; a man looked up to and admired by everybody; a man who can afford to give his wife white bread every day, a gold chain for her neck, a carpet on the floor, and red wine to drink on holidays ; eh, Micheline?

MICHELINE *(looking back at door and curtseying).*—And was that all you had to say to me, sir?

KOULIKOFF.— Not at all! I had just begun. The fact is, that I am thinking about getting married. How does it strike you, Micheline?

MICHELINE *(coquettishly).*— You want a fair answer, neighbor?

KOULIKOFF *(trying to take her hand).*— It will never be so fair as the speaker, pretty one.

MICHELINE *(crosses herself).*— Pray don't, sir ; praises bring ill luck, you know.

KOULIKOFF.— Shall   I   take   this   for   an   answer, Micheline?   *(Offers to kiss her.)*

MICHELINE *(eluding him, boxes his ears and runs to L. D.).*— Take *that* for an answer, you ugly old gray-beard!   *(Exit Micheline, laughing L. D.)*

KOULIKOFF *(rubbing his ear).*— The second to-day ; the jades are all alike. "He that has burnt himself with hot milk, should blow on cold water." This is the last time a woman shall get the better of Koulikoff, I'll swear! By the beard of Beelzebub, I'll not submit to it!

> *(Enter the Baroness Vladimir C. D. F. Koulikoff starts back in dismay and assumes a cringing attitude.*

BARONESS.— What! has my brother not yet arrived?

KOULIKOFF *(at L. obsequiously).*— No, Madame la Baronne.

BARONESS.— Tiresome Gustave ; he always was the most provoking dear fellow in the world. Here have I journeyed all the way from Warsaw on purpose to give him a joyful surprise, and to greet my new sister-in-law, hoping to find a house full of people in honor of the nuptials, and all sorts of gayety. On the contrary, gloom, silence, desertion surround me, and I have to do my own honors. At least, you have news of your master, Intendant?

KOULIKOFF.— No, Madame. The Count has not yet honored his new property by a visit.

BARONESS *(looking around her)*.— Certainly, this is superb. Such a gallery for balls out yonder. The rest of my luggage has been carried to my apartments?

(Koulikoff bows.)

BARONESS *(walking to and fro)*.— And how in the name of wonder, am I to amuse myself until they come? *(Yawns.)* Positively I begin to be stupefied already. Ah! I remember. I am to administer justice, after the fashion of this barbarous region. I am to be the arbiter of Fate in this most romantic of love affairs. Delicious! I had quite forgotten my prisoners and my protégé. It all comes of Stephanie's stupidity in spilling chocolate on my china silk dressing gown. Fly! Intendant, and fetch these people to me. How stupid you were not to have thought of it before.

KOULIKOFF.— If Madame la Baronne pleases, Madame la Baronne did not give me time to think. *(Aside.)* Oh! these fine ladies—— *(Exit ruefully C. D. F.)*

BARONESS.— Koulikoff!

KOULIKOFF *(re-entering)*.— Madame la Baronne!

BARONESS.— Stay a moment, and don't go rushing off like that, when you know I have something to say to you. I—ah—gave the orders for the arrest rather hurriedly, you know, and I don't quite understand the merits of the case.

KOULIKOFF.— Madame la Baronne's orders were quite as hurriedly obeyed, I assure her.

BARONESS.— Don't waste time now, but tell me all about it. As soon as I arrive in my brother's castle, almost before I finish warming my feet, a note is put into my hand, imploring the protection of the Château Woroffski for an innocent young woman against the wrong and perfidy of barbarians who seek to hold her prisoner. I might have lived for years in Paris and nothing so delightful would have occurred. I was in haste, as I remarked before, so I just signed a general order to arrest everybody concerned and hold them until my brother's arrival. This is such a convenient country for that sort of thing !

KOULIKOFF.— It is indeed, Madame la Baronne.

BARONESS.— What do you mean, man ? ·Don't presume to agree with me when I state a general proposition.

KOULIKOFF.— Perhaps Madame would like to examine the witnesses in the case ?

BARONESS *(clasping hands).*— The witnesses—what are they ? Yes, of course. *(Settles herself on sofa R.)* This is exactly like amateur theatricals—without the quarrelling. Bring in your witnesses, Intendant.

> *(Exit Koulikoff L. D. after putting foot stool, etc.*
> *Re-enter Koulikoff followed by Ivan and Micheline L., Koulikoff goes behind sofa R.)*

BARONESS *(disappointed).*— What—that old thing—and a girl of her age ! preposterous ! Well, my good man, and what is the sad story they are telling me about your enticing this poor little creature into a marriage against her will. Fie, for shame ! one wouldn't have expected it of such a respectable looking, venerable old party as you are. By the way, what a capital figure you'd make for a fancy ball ; an elderly Adonis, ha–ha–ha !

IVAN *(L. C. puzzled ; aside).*— Women have long hair

and short wits; says the proverb: but I'm blest if I know what to make of this one.

KOULIKOFF *(L. of sofa).*— Your pardon, Madame, but you are laboring under a misapprehension. This man is not the principal in the case; but only the shoemaker at whose cottage the affair occurred, and the girl is his daughter, Micheline. *(Aside.)* Little viper!

BARONESS *(sharply).*— His daughter; then they are not the right ones, after all. What a dunce you are, Intendant, to have allowed me to think these people were the—ah— principals in the case! They don't amuse me in the least!

IVAN.— If I am permitted to explain in full, my lady——

BARONESS *(yawning).*— Oh, pray don't, my good man. I'm convinced that you are long-winded. People in your class of life always are, you know. Koulikoff, I think, on the whole, I am tired of witnesses. Bring me something else.

KOULIKOFF.— And Madame has, then, no special orders in reference to these prisoners?

BARONESS.— Keep the old man somewhere, and let the girl go to my apartment. I shall try to coax that jealous Stephanie into letting me have her for an under-maid.

IVAN *(aside).*— Takes seven women to make one soul, says the proverb. Whew! only fancy seven like that!
(Exeunt Ivan and Micheline L. D.)

KOULIKOFF.— The wife of Alexis Petrovitch awaits your orders in the ante-chamber, Madame.

BARONESS *(taking up embroidery).*— Show her in at once, man; don't delay, when you know that I am dying of curiosity.

KOULIKOFF *(aside).*— Oh! these fine ladies!
(Exit Koulikoff L. D.)

BARONESS.— I'm actually enjoying myself. Now for the real heroine of this pretty pastoral.

*(Enter Koulikoff L. D. leading Poleska, whose head
is drooping, her eyes cast down.)*

KOULIKOFF *(patronizingly).*— Draw near, my good
woman. Have no fear; Madame la Baronne Vladimir, the
sister and representative of our gracious master, deigns to
receive you and listen to your story.

POLESKA *(turning on him haughtily).*— That will do.
Bring me a seat, and leave us.

KOULIKOFF *(aside).*— Hoity-toity—bring me a seat—the
most refreshing piece of impudence Koulikoff has encoun-
tered yet.

*(He bustles round to back of sofa R. where Baro-
ness sits. Poleska remains standing.)*

POLESKA *(aside bitterly).*— He is right. I forget my sta-
tion.

*(Baroness trifles negligently with her dress, leisurely
adjusts her eye-glass, then bestows a stare upon
Poleska.)*

BARONESS *(aside).*— Upon my word, a remarkably good
looking creature for a peasant! *(Aloud.)* So it appears, my
dear, that you have been trifled with. How very shocking!
For a man to trifle with a woman is to undermine the whole
structure of society. For a woman to trifle with a man is
quite another thing! What is your name?

POLESKA.— Poleska.

BARONESS.— And whence do you come?

POLESKA.— From Buda, in Hungary.

BARONESS.— From Buda! Is it possible? Perhaps, then,
you have chanced to hear of the distinguished General de
Fermstein?

POLESKA *(C. starting, aside).*— My father! Can it be
that she suspects me? *(Aloud.)*, Yes Madame, I knew him
well. I—we—our family owe everything to his goodness.

BARONESS.— How very odd ! Maybe you can give me some tidings of my new sister-in-law. I set out on my annual journey to Paris, just as my brother, the Count Woroffski, was beginning to talk about this beautiful Mlle. de Fermstein, whom he had seen at a ball when in Baden. Like a good sister, I made it my business to find out everything disagreeable I could about the girl; and I assure you it was not difficult. Such tales as they tell of her temper ! Well, I went off to Paris ; and on my return, recently, I received one of my brother's short, unsatisfactory telegrams, informing me that he proposed to marry Mlle. de Fermstein on such a date, and would go to the Château immediately, to pass his honeymoon. I always was an impetuous creature, and my husband, the Baron, decidedly disapproved of the whole business. So that was quite enough to make me start off at a moment's notice and take this long, miserable journey.

POLESKA *(much agitated).*— Oh ! Madame, spare me. I—oh ! *(She bursts into tears, sits L.)*

BARONESS *(glass at eye ; astonished).*— This girl is certainly mad. Young woman, I must beg of you to restrain yourself. I am not accustomed to such emotional demonstrations from people in your rank of life. *(Resumes.)* Of course, under the present circumstances, my feelings towards Mlle. de Fermstein are quite different; I am prepared to meet her as a sister. *(Aside to audience.)* We all know what that means. *(Aloud.)* But that doesn't prevent your telling me any bits of gossip you may have heard about her —something light and spicy—a tiny indiscretion, you know. They do say she was not entirely to blame for her horrible temper. That her father, a weak old fellow, spoiled her from her cradle and worshipped the very ground she trod on.

POLESKA.— Oh, he did—he did. And you are right, she was not worthy of such love—the noblest, truest father that was ever cursed with an unhappy child.

BARONESS *(eagerly)*.— Then you do know something against her? This really becomes exciting.

POLESKA *(rising, with dignity)*.— I know this, Madame, that her worst indiscretion has been bitterly punished by her terrible fate. Yes, Madame la Baronne, I am Poleska de Fernstein; not the wife of your brother, as you and— Heaven help me—as I believed—but the victim of a foul conspiracy, by which I find myself married to a vile usurper of your brother's rank and name. The telegram to you was no doubt part of the plot.

BARONESS.— Can this be possible, Mademoiselle; I mean, Madame?

POLESKA.— Unfortunately, it is. Judge, therefore, whether I, Poleska de Fermstein, have not the right to claim of you and yours protection for myself—and—*(between her teeth)*, punishment for him. *(Goes up stage.)*

BARONESS *(fanning herself and using salts)*.— Horrible, horrible! my dear, you make me really ill! What a blow to society! The villain—to dare to send me a telegram! But pray tell me, child, what sort of a creature is this thief—this outlaw; is he at all a good-looking fellow, perchance?

(Poleska's eyes droop. Baroness turns to Koulikoff
inquiringly. Koulikoff R. of sofa.)

KOULIKOFF.— Y-e-s, Madame la Baronne, I am con-strained to admit that he is not ill-looking, and that he bears himself with astonishing coolness—the rogue. One would think he had been born to command—the scoundrel.

BARONESS.— Indeed? Now, I begin to be really inter-ested. I must have him in, at once. My dear child, set your mind at rest. You are under my care, and if it will give you the least satisfaction, I will order your husband to be hanged upon the spot.

POLESKA *(starting violently, her hand upon her heart).* — Oh ! Madame la Baronne, not that, not that.

BARONESS.— Somebody ought to be hanged, I am sure. Gustave will be very much vexed if I don't hang somebody.

POLESKA.— Then take Ivan, the shoemaker, or your Intendant there. I believe they are both in the plot.

KOULIKOFF *(knees knocking together).*— Good Lord !

POLESKA *(beseechingly).*— All I ask, Madame, is that you will send me back to my father.

BARONESS.— I will do better, my dear child. I will conduct you there myself. What a sensation for society ! Mlle. de Fermstein, the proudest beauty of the Court, married to a serf !

POLESKA.— What humiliation !

BARONESS *(eagerly).*— I declare, I almost wish I were there already, to hear what people will say. But the main thing is, to dissolve the marriage. Of course there will be no difficulty in finding a plea for divorce. He—this Alexis— is rough and brutal ? Violent and cruel, eh ?

POLESKA.— He ? Ah, no, he is gentleness itself.

BARONESS.— Well, then, state your grievance as you please, only be quick about it. *(Poleska remains silent.)*

BARONESS.—Good Heavens ! girl, did I ever before see a wife at a loss for a grievance against her husband ?

KOULIKOFF.— With submission, Madame la Baronne. Madame la Baronne perhaps forgets that the Count himself, without tedious processes of law is able to break the marriage of his serf.

BARONESS.— True ! they manage somethings far better here than in Paris ! How lucky for Mlle. de Fermstein. Go, my dear, into my chamber ; draw up your petition for divorce, sign it and give it to me.   The rest shall be speedily settled.

POLESKA *(reluctantly).*— Y-e-e-s—Madame; but afterwards——

BARONESS *(mimicking Poleska).*— Afterwards? What
do you mean? You are free. You return to your father.
You will never see this wretch again. What more would
you have?

POLESKA.— And he—Gustave—Alexis, I would say—he
will be at liberty to marry—again?

BARONESS.— Certainly, and so will you, my dear, so cheer
up.   *(A knock at L. D.)*

KOULIKOFF *(aside).*—That's the villain, the hero of all
this rumpus. I locked him into the little blue cabinet an
hour ago. *(Aloud.)* I forgot to say Madame la Baronne,
that this man demanded to be shown to your presence, as if
it were his right, confound him.

POLESKA *(going and returning impetuously).*— Ah,
Madame, see him. Talk to him. Console him, tell him I
wish him no further ill, but tell him how unalterable is the
resolution I have taken to see him no more——I mean, the
resolution I am about to take.

> *(Exit Poleska in tears R. D.   Baroness looks after
> her curiously and smiles.)*

BARONESS.— Intendant, produce your prisoner. How
nice it is to administer justice! I am quite in the humor of
the thing. And now to meet this bold, bad man! I must be
as stern and dignified as the situation demands.

>   *(Knocking continues.)*

KOULIKOFF *(going slowly, opens L. D).* What manners
for a jail bird!

> *(Enter Alexis L. D.   Baroness looks up, and utters
> a cry of astonishment, but is met by a warning
> gesture.)*

BARONESS *(aside).*— My brother here, in peasant's garb ? Impossible !

ALEXIS.— Madame la Baronne, I beg of you to require this man to leave us. What I would say to you needs no witness.

KOULIKOFF *(swelling with rage).*— Do you hear that ? Madame la Baronne, I protest.

BARONESS *(without looking at Koulikoff).*— Leave us, fellow !

KOULIKOFF *(to Alexis).*— Leave us, fellow !

ALEXIS *(menacingly).*— Leave *us*, fellow !

(*Koulikoff shrinks back.*)

BARONESS.— Take pens, ink and paper, Koulikoff, to the young lady in my room. Remain outside until candles are required.

KOULIKOFF *(aside.)*— He " fellow " me ! A miserable vassal I shall probably be called upon to knout before bed time. Won't I lay it on for this, though ?

(*Exit Koulikoff R. D.*)

BARONESS *(throwing herself in the arms of Alexis).*— Gustave, my dear brother, you here, in this disguise ! What a comedy ! Oh ! I shall die of laughter !

GUSTAVE.— I don't feel in the least like laughing, Leontine, I assure you. To be cooped up in that stuffy blue cabinet for an hour is no joke.

BARONESS.— This mystery—this adventure—delicious as it is, I don't in the least understand it. You have this moment arrived ?

GUSTAVE.— I have been in the neighborhood for the past three days on business, which involves the happiness of my entire life. And your imprudence, my dear sister, has nearly ruined me—that's all.

BARONESS *(laughing).*— Ruined you ! Are you, then,

the hero of this little romance?   Oh! this is too delicious for anything!   *(Sits.)*

GUSTAVE *(sitting on stool beside Baroness).*— Leontine, I was married to Poleska de Fermstein a week ago.   This is our honeymoon, and already I am the most miserable of men.

BARONESS *(shrugging shoulders).*— Are you surprised at that?   Gustave, dear, I am dying of impatience.   Tell me the story in detail.

GUSTAVE.— You remember, Leontine, when I first fell passionately in love with Mlle. de Fermstein, at a ball in Baden, and without even making her acquaintance, how I told you that she and no other should be my wife?

BARONESS.— Yes, and if I mistake not, I gave you some advice which you religiously failed to appreciate.

GUSTAVE.— Of what use is advice to a man who is in love?   Well, when, upon my next visit to Buda, I was presented to her in form, I rushed more blindly to my fate.   I would have her—I worshipped her madly—I—married her. Alas!   Her arrogance, her pride of rank, her scorn of inferiors are irrepressible.   I soon saw that the welfare of our married life was at stake.   I resolved to cure her; and adopted a heroic remedy.   Poleska's ardent desire to visit our newly acquired estates in this region gave me the opportunity I desired.   Poor Poleska!   It was a bitter cup I offered her to drink!   *(He stops abruptly.)*

BARONESS.— And now, you dear, odd, Quixotic Gustave —and now?

GUSTAVE *(sadly).*— Now, hope has departed.   My wife despises me.

BARONESS.—And it is to your naughty, mischief-making sister you owe the chief part of your trouble.   For had I not sent so promptly to arrest you and your fellow villains, you might by this time have won over your Poleska to regard with complacency her future life spent in a hovel at your side. Ha, ha, ha !

GUSTAVE.— I think she loves me, Leontine—did love me, at least, after her fashion. And as ill luck would have it just as I set the finishing touch to my structure of cards, down came the whole fabric crashing to the ground.

BARONESS *(twirling her fan)*.— Gustave, with all your knowledge of society and of women, you are a very tyro in a matter of this kind. If I were not so sorry for you, poor boy, I should tell you that you deserve all you have got, for making such an experiment ; but I'll be merciful. What if I tell you a secret, Gustave ? What if I whisper in your ear that, in my opinion, Poleska is as much in love with you at this moment as you are with her ?

GUSTAVE.— Leontine ! My darling sister !

BARONESS.— And if I prove it ?

GUSTAVE *(kissing her hand)*.— Ah, Leontine, do not jest with me. Prove it and I forgive all.

(Enter Koulikoff C. D. F. with candle. He stops, with exaggerated gestures of surprise, and backs out discreetly, finger on lip.)

KOULIKOFF *(aside)*.— Making love to the Baroness in ten minutes' time. I'll hurry off and tell his wife. One always likes to be the first to tell exciting news. W-h-e-w !

(Exit C. D. F.)

BARONESS *(archly)*.— In the first place, she was not at all anxious to have you hanged.

GUSTAVE *(shrugging shoulders.)*— Is that all ?

BARONESS.— When I abused you, she took your part ; that might have been through contradiction, to be sure. I have often done so myself. But when I proposed to annul your marriage on the spot, to my surprise she demanded time for reflection.   She wavered—she wept—in short, Gustave, I believe that Poleska is on the brink of offering to share your fortunes, good or ill.

GUSTAVE.— You are in earnest, Leontine?

BARONESS.— For once, yes.   When a pretty woman demands time for reflection, it is safe to assume that she is about to commit a folly.

GUSTAVE.— If I could hope! Oh! my Poleska. Oh! Leontine!   *(Offers to embrace her.)*

BARONESS.— Keep that for Poleska, my dear boy. I know the lover's liturgy by heart.   Hark! some one comes.

   (Enter Koulikoff R. D. pompously, bearing paper.)

KOULIKOFF.— Madame la Baronne, I have the honor to present to you a paper this moment signed and committed to me by Mlle. de Fermstein.

   *(Koulikoff retires up.   Baroness takes it eagerly,
   glances at it and looks with alarm at her brother.
   Gustave takes the paper from her and reads
   it.)*

GUSTAVE.— All is over.   Pride has conquered.   This is the petition for our divorce, signed by Poleska with a firm hand.   Let me not be behind her in courage.

   *(He walks quickly to the table, writes and returns
   paper to the Baroness.)*

GUSTAVE.— You will give this, signed by Gustave, Count de Woroffski, to Mlle. de Fermstein without delay. , Her marriage with Alexis Petrovitch is annulled.   It is my wish that the young lady be returned at once, in a style suitable to her rank, to her father, the General de Fermstein, and that you, Baroness, accompany her.   *(To Koulikiff, aloud.)* Have a carriage made ready, and order servants to be in attendance upon these ladies.

KOULIKOFF *(at C. D. F.)*— And by whose authority, may I ask?

GUSTAVE *(L. stamping foot)*.— By whose authority, varlet? By my—at least—with the gracious permission of Madame la Baronne. What is more, let them set at liberty my late master, Ivan, the shoemaker, with a purse of one hundred roubles, to make amends for his imprisonment.

(Koulikoff looks in astonishment at Baroness.)

BARONESS.— Go, Koulikoff. These are my orders.

(Koulikoff lingers, aghast).

GUSTAVE *(perceiving Koulikoff, angrily)*.— What, still here? Fifty blows of the knout for your own share—at least—with the gracious permission of Madame la Baronne.

(Koulikoff flies in dismay.)

BARONESS *(laying hand on Gustave's shoulder)*.— Gustave, dear, this is dreadful. If you would only see her once again, all would go well, I'm sure.

GUSTAVE.— Enough, Leontine. Go and make ready for your journey. Breathe no word to Poleska of my real rank and condition until you give her to her father's hand. I will prepare for you a letter to him, telling him all. When you have left the Castle, I will announce myself to my people.

(Enter Poleska C. D. F. He leads Baroness to R. D. and parts from her affectionately. Poleska watches them.)

BARONESS *(aside)*.— Thank Heaven, that I am not his wife; and now for woman's wit; one more expedient, before I lay my sceptre down. *(Exit Baroness R. D.)*

POLESKA.— It is true then, and Koulikoff did not deceive me. Already Alexis has sought consolation in another's smiles. *(She comes forward.)*

GUSTAVE *(perceiving Poleska, bows coldly)*.— You have

decreed our separation, Mademoiselle, and the Count has signed the paper. You are freed forever from the tie you found so hateful. In a few moments you will leave behind the Château Woroffski and all the odious memories it contains. Alexis, the serf, passes out of your life like an evil dream, and perchance you will soon form an alliance worthy of your rank and expectations.

POLESKA.— You might have spared me that sneer. You make no account of my blighted life, the scorn and humiliation that await me.

> *(Her head droops and she turns away to hide her tears.)*

GUSTAVE *(quickly)*.— Tears, Poleska? and I have brought them to your eyes. Oh! pardon something to a man mad with the sense of loss. I am mad, I confess it, when I see you go from me, without a token of regret.

> *(He takes her hand. Poleska draws back.)*

POLESKA.— You mistake me for the Baroness, perhaps.

GUSTAVE *(bewildered)*.— What do you mean? Leontine? The Baroness Vladimir? Ridiculous.

POLESKA *(fiercely)*.— I might have pardoned all, Alexis, until I heard from Koulikoff and saw for myself what passed between you and one till now a stranger.

GUSTAVE *(aside)*.— Jealous! Thank Heaven! *(Aloud.)* What you saw, Poleska, was no exhibition of mere gallantry, but of gratitude from the bottom of my heart to a noble lady who had promised to win back my wife for me. Now the protection she has offered me will avail little. Let the Count's sentence be what it may, fate can give me nothing worse than this.

POLESKA *(at L.)*.— Sentence! Great Heavens! Alexis, are they going to do anything to you?

GUSTAVE.— You can hardly suppose that the Count de

Woroffski will allow to pass unpunished such audacity in his serf? Stripes, banishment, death perhaps.

(Alexis withdraws to chair at table R. drops his head moodily on his hands without looking towards her.)

POLESKA *(screams).*— Death— Oh ! Alexis —never ! never ! Let us escape together. I love you ! I *cannot live without you !*

(She crosses the stage and throws herself on her knees at his side.)

GUSTAVE *(lifting her to her feet, clasping her in his arms, then putting her from him).*— Think twice, Poleska. He whose fortune you would share is no proud Count, but an humble peasant, and the life to which you would go, a life of toil and poverty.

POLESKA.— Let me fly, Alexis—no matter where, so that you are with me. Every moment's delay will endanger you.

(They hurry towards C. D. F. and push it open to be met by Koulikoff, Ivan, Micheline, guards, and servants.)

KOULIKOFF *(to guards).*— Arrest that fellow, and conduct him without delay into the Count's chamber to await his sentence from Madame la Baronne. As for you, Mlle. de Fermstein, your carriage waits, and Madame la Baronne desires your immediate attendance in her chamber.

POLESKA *(her arm in that of Alexis).*— Say to Madame la Baronne that I prefer to remain with my husband.

KOULIKOFF *(extending paper).*— Begging your pardon, Mlle. de Fermstein, you haven't any husband. Here is your decree of absolute divorce which Madame la Baronne directs me to hand to you. Move on, prisoner.

*(Gustave goes out C. D. F. with guards; Poleska
remains with arms outstretched towards him.)*

MICHELINE.— Oh, Madame, then they mean to make
you a great lady once more whether you will or not.

KOULIKOFF.— And pray what business have you to
prate, malapert? The Count's word is our law, and what
the law decrees, let none gainsay.

MICHELINE *(scornfully).*— And does the law expect her
to forget her poor young husband in exile and in sorrow?
For after all, she wants him for her husband, and he wants
her for his wife, and the law can't alter that, I suppose?

KOULIKOFF.— Hum! I'm not so sure. Lawyers are
very clever.

MICHELINE *(to Poleska, who is weeping upon her shoulder).*— Ah! Madame, cheer up! who knows but there are
brighter days in store for you? If we could only manage to
offer a big rouble taper to our Lady of Kazan! Why—last
week when I had quarrelled with Osip at the Fair, I set two
little copeck candles only, before her shrine, and—and, the
foolish lad was back again by Sunday.

IVAN *(coming forward).*— Come, come, chatterbox. So
our would-be Countess takes the opposite side. That's the
way with you women. If I ever told my old woman to get
up early, she'd lie abed three days at a stretch. If I wanted
her to go to sleep, she'd sit on the stove and wag her tongue
till daybreak. *(Movement of disgust from Poleska.)*

MICHELINE.— Let be, let be, father; the poor thing has
trouble enough, dear knows.

(Enter Baroness R. D. dressed for traveling.)

BARONESS.— Come, Mlle de Fermstein, my dear, this will
never do. You have absolutely left yourself no time to return to the garb of civilization. Micheline here, will attend
you. Do go and make yourself presentable for our journey.

POLESKA.— No, dear Madame; if you will only give me back Alexis I will never wear another dress than this.

BARONESS.— My dear child, this is simply ridiculous. You are soon to be away from this wretch who has deceived you. You will meet some other more worthy of your love; and together, one day, you will laugh at the poor fool who once risked his life to win you.

POLESKA.— Oh, Madame, have pity on me. Do you not see that I love him, that my only happiness would be to follow him to exile?

IVAN.— Well, as I'm a free man with a hundred roubles in my pocket, I do believe she wants him back again.

MICHELINE.— Of course she does, father, and small blame to her, poor dear.

BARONESS *(to Poleska, coldly)*.— Did you not, of your own free will, demand this separation?

POLESKA.— Oh, I did, I did, in a moment of madness. Madame, you are a woman; you can understand.

IVAN.—If she can, I can't.

MICHELINE *(sighing)*.— I can. *(Wiping her eyes.)* He's a beautiful young man.

BARONESS.— I have no longer the right. My brother has returned; the matter has passed into his hands. The Count is at this moment going into the gallery to give audience to his vassals. Stop crying, child, you will make a fright of yourself. If you say so, although it is contrary to custom, I will send word for him to come here. You will see what a brother I have—so grand—so noble—and above all, so just. What say you? Shall I send for him?

POLESKA.— Yes. Stay! What shall I do? What say to him?

BARONESS.— Whatever your heart prompts.

POLESKA.— Do you think he will be merciful ; that he will give me back Alexis ?

BARONESS.— Perhaps.   He has a very feeling heart.

POLESKA.— Then send for him.   On my knees will I implore him.

BARONESS *(goes to table, writes hurriedly, rings bell; enter attendant R. D.).*— See that the Count Woroffski receives this, at once.   *(Exit attendant R. D.)*

KOULIKOFF— The Count !   He has arrived without my knowing it.   Let me fly in search of my keys.

> *(Exit Koulikoff C. D. F.   March music heard back.)*

BARONESS *(to Poleska.)*— He is coming !   Remain there. *(Points to back.)*   When I summon you to come forward— you know the rest.

> *(Poleska retires back.   Enter peasants and servants. Groups right and left.   Baroness Vladimir goes about, receives greetings and salutes.   Last of all, enter Gustave, Count de Woroffski, dressed in rich uniform, with orders, etc.   March ceases. Soft music during this scene.)*

GUSTAVE.— You sent for me, Madame la Baronne ?

BARONESS.— I did.   *(Aside to him.)*   Hope !   Love has conquered.

GUSTAVE *(aside).*— Thank Heaven !

> *(Baroness motions to Poleska, who comes forward, and without looking up throws herself upon her knees as the Count approaches.)*

POLESKA *(offering paper).*— Count de Woroffski, I beseech you to destroy this fatal paper, divorcing me from Alexis Petrovitch.   I retract my appeal for separation.   Whatever be his sentence I ask you to let me share it.   He is good and noble, and he has my whole heart.   I only, through my wicked folly, have exposed him to this degradation, and my life's love shall atone for the wrong I have done him.

(The Count impetuously tears the paper and throws it away.)

GUSTAVE.— And should I condemn him and you to exile ?

POLESKA *(kissing his hand)*.— Thanks, my lord Count ; a thousand thanks. Add one thing only to your bounty ; restore to me my husband.

GUSTAVE *(C.)*.— Look up, Poleska, he is here.

(Poleska looks up, utters a cry and flies into his embrace.)

BARONESS *(at L. C.)*.— It is your sister's turn now, Poleska. *(They embrace.)* It is true that I hardly expect to be forgiven for my share in Gustave's experiment, though there is one thing to comfort you, my child ; you will have henceforth, every opportunity to punish him as he deserves.

POLESKA *(R. C.)*.— I, Madame la Baronne ?

BARONESS *(laughing)*.— Yes, for is he not your husband ?

(Enter Koulikoff L. D. in haste and confusion, bearing the keys of the Castle on a tray. He kneels with great humility before the Count.)

KOULIKOFF.— Monseigneur, I, your Intendant. *(Looks up.)* Good Lord ! the insolent vassal——!

COUNT.— Yes, Koulikoff, the same, who, in this moment of supreme happiness, is weak enough to forgive you the knouting you deserve—at least—*(glances at Baroness)*, with the gracious permission of Madame——

BARONESS *(motioning towards Poleska)*.— Of Madame la Comtesse.   *(Koulikoff retires in confusion.)*

COUNT.— Come hither, friend Ivan, shoemaker and philosopher. What! not even a proverb ready to answer me with? *(Slaps him on shoulder.)* As for little Micheline, the sooner she finds a husband, the larger dowry will I bestow on her.

> *(Micheline kisses Poleska's hand gratefully. As she retires, Ivan pats her head, calls up Osip and joins their hands in dumb show.)*

COUNT.— And now, Poleska, if any one should tremble, it is I. How can you ever pardon me?

POLESKA *(archly)*.— You forget that Monseigneur has already pardoned my Alexis.

COUNT *(kneeling at her feet)*.— Then may Poleska pardon Monseigneur.

Curtain.